# Dear Mr. President™

**Abraham Lincoln**
Letters from a Slave Girl

by Andrea Davis Pinkney

WINSLOW PRESS

Florida • New York

DISCOVER *DEAR MR. PRESIDENT*'S INTERACTIVE
WEB SITE WITH WORLDWIDE LINKS, GAMES, ACTIVITIES,
AND MORE AT **WINSLOWPRESS.COM**

Winslow Press wishes to acknowledge the Library of Congress for the photographs and prints in this book.

DEAR MR. PRESIDENT ™ and the DEAR MR. PRESIDENT ™ logo are registered trademarks of Winslow Press.

Thanks to R. Sean Wilentz, Dayton-Stockton Professor of History and Director, Program in American Studies, Princeton University, for evaluating the manuscript.

Library of Congress Cataloging-in-Publication Data
Pinkney, Andrea Davis.
Abraham Lincoln: letters from a slave girl / by Andrea Davis Pinkney.
p. cm.—(Dear Mr. President)
Includes biographical references and index.
Summary: A fictional correspondence between President Abraham Lincoln and a twelve-year-old slave girl that discusses his decision to write the Emancipation Proclamation.
ISBN: 1-890817-60-0
Lincoln, Abraham, 1809–1865—Juvenile Fiction. [1. Lincoln, Abraham 1809–1865—Fiction. 2. Emancipation Proclamation. 3. Slavery—Fiction. 4. Letters—Fiction.] I. Title. II. Series

PZ7.P6333 Af2001
[fic]—dc21
00-043846

Creative Director: Bretton Clark
Designer: Victoria Stehl
Editor: Margery Cuyler

Printed in U.S.A.
First edition, 05/01

2  4  6  8  10  9  7  5  3  1

Home Office:                   All inquiries:
770 East Atlantic Ave.         115 East 23rd Street
Suite 201                      10th Floor
Delray Beach, FL 33483         New York, NY 10010

WINSLOW PRESS

DISCOVER *DEAR MR. PRESIDENT*'S INTERACTIVE
WEB SITE WITH WORLDWIDE LINKS, GAMES, ACTIVITIES,
AND MORE AT WINSLOWPRESS.COM

*To Susan Snedeker*
—A.D.P

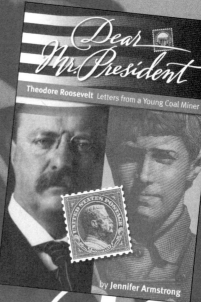
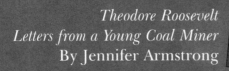

# A Note From the Publisher

This book is our third in the *Dear Mr. President* series. The text is in the form of letters exchanged between President Abraham Lincoln and Lettie Tucker, a young slave girl living on a plantation in Charleston, South Carolina. Although the letters are fictional, the information in them is based on meticulous research. In an effort to capture President Lincoln's personality as well as the life of a young slave girl on a plantation and details on the Civil War, the author relied on a number of reputable books, including *Slavery Time When I Was Chillun, With Malice Toward None: A Life of Abraham Lincoln*, and *The Life and Writings of Abraham Lincoln*, as well as Web sites such as historyplace.com. A list of recommended reading can be found on pages 119–121.

It is our hope that the *Dear Mr. President* books will provide readers with valuable insights into important moments of American history. Each title, written by a skilled author, is further enhanced by interactive footnotes, games, activities, and links, with detailed historical information at the book's own Web site in our virtual library at winslowpress.com.

By offering a rich reading experience coupled with an interactive Web site, we encourage readers to embrace the future with what is best from the past.

**Diane F. Kessenich,** CEO and Publisher, Winslow Press

*President Lincoln at the Fifth Corps headquarters near Sharpsburg, Maryland, 1862*

*Dear Mr. President,*

Yours for true,

Lettie Tucker

Dear Lettie Tucker,

Sincerely,

*A. Lincoln*

When the first shots of the Civil War were fired in 1861, America entered one of the most turbulent periods in its history. The nation had become divided against itself. The Confederates in the South wanted to uphold an economy which was largely dependent on cotton and tobacco farming. This way of life could not exist easily without the institution of slavery. Northerners in the Union states eagerly sought to modernize through industry and wage labor. Many Northerners viewed slavery as a violation of human rights, and stood firmly against it.

Slavery was at the core of the war between the states, and throughout the war's four years, the issue of slavery was a hotbed of controversy. Would the Civil War's outcome put an end to this injustice? Or would the South prevail and allow slavery to remain an evil and corroding thread that wound through the nation's tapestry?

President Abraham Lincoln had been in office a mere five weeks when the Civil War began. His primary concern was not to end slavery, but rather to contain it in the states that already upheld it. That way, he hoped to preserve the Union as it had been structured up until that time. But as the war progressed, it became apparent to the president that slavery was central to the war's outcome. Lincoln came to see that abolishing slavery, which he believed was a moral injustice, would also weaken the South and cause the Confederacy's eventual downfall.

When the president wrote a draft of the Emancipation Proclamation and read it to his cabinet on September 22, 1862, word spread that he would issue the final and official document on New Year's Day, 1863, which would call for the freedom of all slaves in the Southern rebel states.

Once it was known that President Lincoln intended to wipe out slavery, his Emancipation Proclamation became a source of speculation and debate. His declaration was especially important to the enslaved men, women, and children whose very souls were affected daily by slavery's ugly ways. Even though the Emancipation Proclamation did not, in itself, end all slavery, it ignited the spark for slavery's final demise, which came at the end of the Civil War, when the Thirteenth Amendment was ratified on January 31, 1865.

Though it was illegal and dangerous for slaves to learn to read and write, many did become proficient readers and writers. And many took it upon themselves to write directly to the president, expressing their frustrations about the war and their hopes and dreams for becoming free citizens.

Imagine a slave girl named Lettie Tucker living on a plantation in Charleston, South Carolina. Imagine her having to secretly learn to read and write, although it was not legal and would put a slave in jeopardy to do either. Imagine her courage in sending a letter to President Abraham Lincoln, the sixteenth president of the United States.

(Left) A howitzer gun captured by Butterfield's Brigade near Hanover Courthouse, May 27, 1862. (Right) Background: A group of slaves in Cumberland Landing, Virginia, 1862, photograph by J. F. Gibson

To learn more about the causes of the Civil War, visit winslowpress.com.

Dear Mr. President Abraham Lincoln,

My mama once told me that I will know when the world is coming to an end. She says Armageddon is near when smoke paints the sky. When thunder booms loud enough to shake the trees. When fire lights the day.

Mr. President, just three days ago at day clean, I truly believed the world did not have much time left. All the signs of damnation had come right here to Charleston. There was smoke, black as ash, rising high off the harbor. There were flashes of fire. There were strange, sudden blasts that put a hurt to my ears. I stood and watched from the pier.

Soon as I saw the fire, I asked the Almighty to prepare me for judgment day. You see, Mr. President, I am a right and proper Christian, and I am hoping for a place in Heaven. Seeing as it appeared my time had come, I wanted to be ready.

Days later, after the noise and smoke had cleared, word came to us of a war startin'. Folks have been calling it a war to restore national unity. And they're saying it is a war to end slavery.

With all this hearsay going around, I now got a bees' nest of questions buzzing up inside me. I figure you, Mr. President, being the highest officer in our land, can answer my questions better than anyone. I have put my questions to paper, in the hopes to find out the truth.

What is this war? Will this war turn back the giant wheel of slavery? 'Cause if this be a fact, I will not have to wait for the end of the world to find heaven.

Yours for true,

*Lettie Tucker*

**Tucker Plantation, Charleston, South Carolina**

**To see a time line of the Civil War, visit winslowpress.com.**

*(Left) A slave gathering sugar cane on an Alabama plantation. (Right) A view of Meeting Street, looking south toward the Circular Church, the Mills House, and St. Michael's Church, Charleston, South Carolina, 1865*

**May 23, 1861**

**Executive Mansion, Washington**

Dear Lettie Tucker,

I received your correspondence and read it with great interest. I will do my best to answer your questions.

Indeed, a war has begun. This war's unfortunate start was ignited when General Pierre G. T. Beauregard's Confederate forces attacked the U.S. Army post at Fort Sumter in the harbor of Charleston. Surrounded by rebel batteries, Major Robert Anderson was forced to surrender.

There are many parts to this war, but mostly, as with any war, this one is about differences. Plainly put, the Confederates in the South want more than anything to preserve their agricultural way of life. This way of life depends on owning slaves. We who live in the North—the Union—are looking to bring on more modern ways of doing things. We want to industrialize. We're supporters of free labor. Many of us feel slavery is a total violation of the sacred right of a man to govern himself, guaranteed by the Declaration of Independence.

My primary responsibility in the office of president, however, is to preserve the Union as a whole. The Founding Fathers struggled for a great principle, to give liberty, not alone to the people of this country, but hope to the world for all future time. This is why we must save the Union—to preserve that noble promise for all succeeding generations.

I am most distressed that this war is a war between the states. It is a war that has divided our nation against itself, and the burden of achieving unity weighs heavily upon me.

Now, I hope you will oblige me by answering some of my questions. Of what great interest is this war to you? Perhaps you should not encumber your mind with such troubling issues. It is of watered silk and lace flounces that a fine lady should concern herself. War is the ugly work of men.

I wonder about your abilities to articulate so precisely. Your command of the written word shows you have been well-schooled.

Finally, I am curious about your name. I find the name Lettie intriguing, as it is not familiar to me. Is Lettie a sobriquet that stands for a longer name, such as Elizabeth or Ellen?

Sincerely and respectfully,

*A. Lincoln*

A. Lincoln

---

*(Left) Fort Sumter before the war, oil painting by Seth Eastman. (Right) Fort Sumter after the war, oil painting by Seth Eastman*

**To learn more about the secession of Southern states, visit winslowpress.com.**

**To learn more about the attack on Fort Sumter, visit winslowpress.com.**

*Dear Mr. President Abraham Lincoln,*

*The words of your letter brought a smile to every bit of me, first, by calling me a fine lady. Second, by puttin' me in the same company as watered silk and lace flounces.*

*I have been called all sorts of things, but nobody has ever called me fine. I ain't exactly no lady, neither. Ladies are fully growed women-folk who drink sweet tea and sample crullers. And ladies is white women. I am not fully growed, or white.*

*I am the property of Mistress Katherine Tucker, daughter to Master Cyrus Tucker, owner of the Tucker Plantation and the owner of me, my mama and pap, and my little brother Elias. Master Tucker is what my pap calls a Confederate loon— somebody who's crazy about the South.*

*Mistress Katherine, she's a true lady, and she and I have a liking for each other. I have knowed my mistress all my life. And all my life I have called her by her nickname, Missy Kat.*

*Missy Kat put a quill in my hand when I was no higher than the gatepost that marks the edge of Tucker land. Secretly, she showed me how to read and make letters, all by myself. I been knowin' the ways of writing since as long as I can remember.*

*Missy Kat says she can't wait to get her hands on Elias, my little brother. Elias is five years old. He ain't no bigger than a haycock. He's still learning to lift a bucket, and gather night crawlers for fishing bait. Missy Kat says she'll start him in on letters when he's seven. Even though Elias is wide-eyed as a hooty owl, he's much too up-jumpy to sit still for learning letters.*

*I guess you can say I been well-schooled. I have taken to writing somethin', somehow, every single day of my twelve years. I often scratch my name in the black dirt out back by the plantation-house rose garden. I like writing. Missy Kat says I am very good at writing. Missy Kat never lies.*

*It was Missy Kat who gave me a good strong nudge to put*

my thoughts to paper and send them to you. I told Missy Kat I had no business writing to the president. But Missy Kat would not let up. She stayed on me to write you letters. She promised to post the letters for me, as if she was the one sending them. She told me my refusal to write to you was an attitude of defeat before victory.

Now that I have heard from you, I will keep with writing letters. I showed your letter to Missy Kat.

Yours for true,

*Lettie Tucker*

Lettie Tucker

**Tucker Plantation, Charleston, South Carolina**

P.S. My name is just plain Lettie. It don't stand for nothin' but what it is.

*Background: South Carolina plantation, 1857.*
*Slave cabins, 1864*

**Executive Mansion, Washington**

Dear Lettie Tucker,

Your letter both delighted and surprised me. I am pleased to make your acquaintance, if only by post. I would be a dishonest man, however, if I did not express my concern for the fact that you are a Negro girl.

Just a fortnight ago, Southern troops slaughtered Union fighters in Manassas, Virginia, at a creek called Bull Run. It was a bloody battle that ended in a sobering defeat for our Union troops. With more than 500 Union men killed and more than 2,500 wounded or missing, it is clear that there are many days of fighting ahead.

Those who believe slavery is right are zealots for their cause. Daily I receive missives from them in which they demand my execution or wish me thrown into the fires of Hell! Mrs. Lincoln is deeply worried, but I comfort her with the thought that assassination would solve nothing, since the scourge of hatred against Negroes has been unleashed and would remain even if the president were killed.

Lettie, since reading and writing is illegal for Negroes, I must caution you about writing to me. If, somehow in transport, your letters to me were to be discovered, you and your mistress could suffer grave danger.

My secretaries routinely shield me from the quantity of mail I get. As your letters are not official correspondence, I worry that I may not receive some of them.

Though I admire your bravery in writing to me, let us make a pact. Have your mistress address your letters to my son William Wallace Lincoln. My secretaries wouldn't take it upon themselves to open Willie's mail. I have told Willie of our correspondence. You and Willie are close in age and share common interests. Willie is eleven years old. He has a

To learn more about the major battles of the Civil War, visit winslowpress.com.

To learn more about the laws preventing slaves from reading and writing, visit winslowpress.com.

hefty appetite for writing and reading. Though your letters are intended for me, Willie will find a sure pleasure in receiving letters addressed to him.

Despite the many risks we face in writing each other, it is Willie who has encouraged me to maintain a correspondence with you. He says that as president, I should acquaint myself with all Americans, even young people, and even those who are enslaved. Also, Willie knows how much writing relaxes me. I'm sure this is one of the reasons he's urged me to carry on.

When suitable, I would like to share your letters with Willie.

If at any time, however, your well-being becomes threatened for the writing of these letters, I implore you to stop writing them immediately. No one wishes more than I to see a young girl such as you express herself so freely and so well. If this war results in the end of slavery, you will be truly free to voice your opinions. For now, though, vigilance is necessary to our correspondence.

Most sincerely,

A. Lincoln

*Lithograph showing the Union Army's retreat from the Battle of Bull Run, July 21, 1861*

Dear Mr. President Abraham Lincoln,

Writing is the only freedom I got. Missy Kat has agreed to address my letters to your son Willie. But I will not stop writing the letters. I thank you for your concern of my well-being. However, my well-being is most threatened by silence.

You may share my letters with Willie anytime you want.

Yours for true,

*Lettie Tucker*

Lettie Tucker
**Tucker Plantation**
**Charleston, South Carolina**

P.S. Same way as you want me to address my letters to your boy, you should post your letters to my mistress, Katherine Potts Tucker. Up to now, Missy Kat has been giving me your letters before anybody else sees my name on the front of them.

**To learn more about generals of the Civil War, visit winslowpress.com.**

*(Right) General John Charles Frémont. Lincoln viewed his proclamation as an unauthorized political act.*

# September 7, 1861

**Executive Mansion, Washington**

Dear Lettie Tucker,

For a girl of only twelve years, you possess a powerful dose of conviction. I respect that.

I must cut short this letter, as I'm recovering from a visit paid to me by Jessie Frémont, the high-spirited wife of General Frémont, who on 30 August issued a proclamation in the state of Missouri that all slaves were to be set free. This, despite my orders that his proclamation be modified beforehand, as it only serves to alienate our Southern friends. Jessie Frémont is very perturbed with me!

I look forward to receiving more letters from you.

In highest regard,

*A. Lincoln*

A. Lincoln

Dear Mr. President Abraham Lincoln,

I get my conviction from knowing Missy Kat. Keeping my family together was Missy Kat's doing. That girl has got her pa wound tight around that dainty white pinkie of hers. When she wants something from him, she stays with it till he gives in.

All Missy Kat has to do is talk to Master Tucker like she's talkin' to a kitten, and he turns to butter on a hot griddle. Missy Kat's mama died while birthing her. Missy Kat is fifteen, and Master Tucker's only child. She has made gettin' her way something as high styled as ringlet curls.

When Missy Kat turned ten, her pa told her she could choose her birthday gift. She picked only one thing. She made her pa promise he would never sell off me or Mama, Pap, or Elias.

It was at her birthday party that she did this. In front of everyone, she asked her pa to raise his right hand and swear on his promise. I was just a little girl then, but I remember the whole thing like it happened last Tuesday. Mama had baked a birthday cake for Missy Kat and her friends. I helped Mama hand out the dessert forks while I watched Missy Kat work her pa the way Mama works bread dough.

I can still see Master Tucker pushing out a tight little laugh while he made his promise to Missy Kat.

I learned two good lessons that day. One is, when you want to get your way, talk to your pa real soft. (This works for me nowadays.) And, when you want somebody to truly do as they say, make sure other folks is nearby to hear them make their promise.

Master Tucker has kept to his word ever since that day, near to five years back. I am a lucky girl. There is not one other slave child on all of the Tucker Plantation who has both their mama, their pap, and their brother—all the whole family—still living with them. Most colored families on Tucker's place are all broke up. This is the ugly way of slavery—the people you love being selled off, or killed in trying to escape.

I will always be thankful to Missy Kat for what she done for me and mine.

I'm sorry you are so weighed down by all the cares of your office.

Yours for true,

*Lettie Tucker*

Lettie Tucker
**Tucker Plantation**
**Charleston, South Carolina**

*Background: Plantation slaves*

To learn more about how slave families were split apart, visit winslowpress.com.

# October 4, 1861

**Executive Mansion, Washington**

Dear Lettie Tucker,

It seems you and Missy Kat know what wiles to employ to influence your fathers. Children are clever that way. When I told Willie your letters to me would be addressed to him, he asked how he was to be compensated for the use of his name. I suggested a new bridle for his pony. He flatly refused. The bridle he has is sufficient, he said.

Then Willie suggested I allow him to chart the pattern of the stars, using the telescope I reserve for just that purpose. I have agreed to this.

I cannot help but secretly applaud Willie for his tenacity and his powers of persuasion.

I have three sons in all. Robert, age 18, recently won admission to Harvard University. Robert is smart, but at times lacks motivation (he failed the Harvard entrance exam on his first try). My youngest son, Tad, is eight years old. Tad is a delightful child, though he was born with an unfortunate affliction. He has a cleft palate, which causes him to speak improperly.

Willie is the most cunning of my three boys. Upon the arrival of your next letter, I will be obliged to let Willie observe the constellations with the help of my telescope.

Sincerely yours,

*A. Lincoln*

A. Lincoln

**To learn more about Lincoln's children, visit winslowpress.com.**

*Abraham Lincoln and son Thomas "Tad," February 9, 1864, photograph by Matthew B. Brady*

# October 19, 1861

*Dear Mr. President Abraham Lincoln,*

*Appears to be, you are a daddy who loves his young'uns. My mama says family is the honey that sweetens life's bitter times. And believe me, Mama knows all there is to know about sweets. She is the head cook on the Tucker Plantation. Fixin' cakes, pies, gingerbreads, and jams is her special gift. Mama's hands are as strong and as black as horseshoe iron. But they're soft too. Soft in the care she puts to her baking.*

*Even though my ma is not a field slave, she works hard as anybody. She rises way before the sun, so's she can get to Master Tucker's kitchen long before he wakes. And Mama's day don't never seem to end. She got a barrelful of onions and potatoes peeled, chopped, and boiling before most folks is even thinkin' about morning. When I work 'longside Mama in the kitchen—rolling dough, coring apples, shucking corn— Mama don't never seem to stop. Always on her feet, Mama is— from the larder to gather the dried goods, to the cookin' flame to stir broth, to the scullery, where she scrubs ladles, sieves, and the stew pots.*

*Some nights, Mama don't even come back to the slave quarters to sleep. She sleeps on a sawdust palette in the corner of the kitchen, so's she can stay on top of her work.*

*The same is true for my pap. He wakes when the master say wake. Works when the master say work. Sleeps when the master say sleep.*

*Slave dressed in her Sunday best*

To learn more about daily life on a plantation, visit winslowpress.com.

*Mr. Lincoln, if ever you doubted the know-all of nigras, you should meet my pap. Pap is a smart man. Pap is a kind man, too. He knows about trees, flowers, tobacco, and all the things growing on the Almighty's green earth. Pap can bring even the sickliest plants back to full health. And, like Mama, sometimes Pap is workin' even when everybody else sleeps. At night, it's Pap's job to watch for critters that creep up to the henhouse.*

*Master Tucker says Pap is valuable. A true commodity, he calls him. I do not know nothin' about what no commodity is, but it must be good if it has to do with Pap.*

*Mama and Pap don't know letters, but they each got an understanding of things that not even books can teach.*

*Please thank Willie for receiving my letters.*

Yours for true,

*Lettie Tucker*

Lettie Tucker
**Tucker Plantation**
**Charleston, South Carolina**

*P.S. I overheard Master Tucker remark that the Union armies are run by a bunch of cowards. I bit my tongue, although I wanted to tell him I was sure he was wrong.*

# November 2, 1861

**Executive Mansion, Washington**

Dear Lettie Tucker,

I have no doubts about the intelligence of your people. My wife's very own dressmaker is a lovely Negro woman. Elizabeth Keckley is her name. Her creations for Mrs. Lincoln are works of high artistic skill.

Mrs. Lincoln favors jewel tones (she says these accentuate her dark hair and eyes) and florals (these do her proportions justice, I believe). I enclose here a swatch from Elizabeth Keckley's latest sewing remains. It is a sampling of crimson silk. In Elizabeth's hands, this fine fabric will become the gown Mary will wear to a Christmas party at the home of Vice President Hannibal Hamlin. Though I send only a tiny scrap, it is a fragment of proof that Negroes, enslaved or free, possess abilities to be admired.

Mrs. Lincoln has been refurbishing the White House in time for the Christmas season. She is particularly proud of a 700-piece set of Bohemian cut glass that she purchased while on one of her shopping trips north. But I have to confess to having little time to spend with her, since the war takes up most of my waking hours.

Your mother and father seem to be very special people. The remark you overheard from your master is not far from the truth. There has been an alarming lack of action on behalf of our Northern troops!

Sincerely yours,

*A. Lincoln*

A. Lincoln

---

To learn more about Vice President Hannibal Hamlin, visit winslowpress.com.

*Mary Todd Lincoln dressed in finery*

# November 16, 1861

*Dear Mr. President Abraham Lincoln,*

*There ain't no kind of words to tell my feelings for the piece of silk you sent. To me, it ain't no tiny scrap. It is a bolt of joy!*

*You are right. Mama and Pap are very special. It's a wonder, though, that my ma and my pa have so much goodness in them. Mama and Pap have both suffered badly. They don't shy back from tellin' me and Elias about their lives when they was young'uns. Mama says Elias and me need to know how truly wicked slavery is, since Master Tucker ain't as bad as some masters can be.*

*Mama came to the Tucker Plantation when she was no more older than me. Master Tucker bought Mama from the Welty Plantation in Louisiana as a wedding gift for his wife, Missy Kat's mama. Louisiana is what Pap calls cotton country, the way-deep South where masters are meaner than the devil himself.*

*Mama says she was a feisty child, something Master Welty hated. Once, Mama swiped a lump of sugar from Mistress Welty's tea tray, and tucked the sugar in her pocket. When the mistress found the sugar, she made sure Mama was taught a lesson. She had all ten of Mama's fingernails cut out by their roots! To this day, Mama's fingers are all skin. Mama can't scratch herself, no matter how bad she itches.*

*Pap, he came here from the Pendelton Plantation in Virginia. He was sold at auction, just like Mama. Pap don't talk much about his days at the Pendelton place. He don't have to. Pap's bare back tells what he won't.*

*Pap's got bullwhip scars that go from behind his neck to his elbows to right where his pants meet his hips. Them scars is like* tree roots buried underneath the dirt. They are twisted-up ropes of skin. They are truly ugly. It hurts me just to look at them.

Mama and Pap met here at Tucker's. Mama says their love was a right-away thing. When they asked Master Tucker if they could jump the broom, he let them marry.

Mama once said that even though she don't got fingernails for scratchin', the Almighty put a gift right into her hands the very day she met Pap.

It must be hard to have the war on your mind all the time, especially since it keeps you from spending time with your very own wife.

Yours for true,

*Lettie Tucker*

Lettie Tucker
**Tucker Plantation**
**Charleston, South Carolina**

To learn more about slave weddings, visit winslowpress.com.

# December 8, 1861

**Executive Mansion, Washington**

Dear Lettie Tucker,

Your description of the horrors faced by your parents gives me serious pause. Sometimes I try, however falteringly, to put myself in a colored man's shoes. When I do this exercise, I am immediately brought up short, as I remember that many enslaved people don't even have the luxury of owning shoes. There is no way I can fully fathom the disgrace of slavery. But, at the very least, I can imagine a nation free of the laws that uphold its injustice.

I am pleased to know the fabric I sent gladdened you. We should all take pleasure in simple gifts. Elizabeth is putting the finishing touches on my wife's gown. The gown is a lovely sight.

As much as I love Mrs. Lincoln, she suffers at times with ill emotions. Elizabeth's gowns lift her spirits. As this newest gown's beauty is one that inspires, Mary will enjoy the admiration—and envy—it brings. The gown is a holiday gift to anyone who views it.

In just a few days Robert will be home, which will bring joy to his mother's heart—and mine.

Sincerely yours,

*A. Lincoln*

A. Lincoln

*(Left) Mary Todd Lincoln in one of her beautiful dresses. (Right) Robert Todd Lincoln, at about age 25*

**To learn more about Mary Todd Lincoln,** visit winslowpress.com.

Dear Mr. President Abraham Lincoln,

This has been my best Christmas ever. As usual, Mama woke when the sky was still black. But today she didn't rush off to the big house. She stayed right here in the quarters, and set out to making our Christmas supper.

Most every slave on Tucker's place is laid off from working on Christmas. It is the one day each year we can call our own. We started this day with singing and praying, and then, at twelve o'clock, we ate us a supper fit to kill. It was yams, collards, hominy, and pig's knuckles. And Mama baked sweet apples for me and Elias.

Pap's gift to me was a dahlia root-bulb. That bulb ain't nothing but a hard, brown clump. Elias said it is as ugly a Christmas present as anybody could get. I had to explain to that boy that root-bulbs ain't what they seem to be. Outside, they are ugly. Inside, they hold bright and pretty promises. Pap showed me how to tuck the bulb in a croaker sack, then store the sack away in a dark, dry corner. Soon as spring comes, we'll plant the bulb and wait for it to bloom a flower.

Pap's present to Elias was a set of blowing quills, a row of whistles made from reeds. Elias blew those quills all day! All he could make was crooked noises, but everyone danced the turkey trot and the buzzard lope as if they was stepping to fine music.

Since spring is still a ways off, I will have to wait to get the full happiness of my dahlia bulb. Pap says the bulb reminds him of me. He says I'm soon to blossom, but that I have to wait on that, too.

Waiting don't never come easy. Merry Christmas.

Yours for true,

*Lettie*

Lettie
**Tucker Plantation, Charleston, South Carolina**

To learn more about Christmas during
the Civil War, visit winslowpress.com.

*Dancing at a Christmas party,
card drawing, ca. 1863*

# January 5, 1862

**Executive Mansion, Washington**

Dear Lettie Tucker,

Though I am content to let things happen in their own time, I, too, struggle with being patient. Why is it that all that is beautiful and good in life takes time to come to fruition?

Take this war, for example. If its outcome favors the Union, our nation will be a better place. But there is no end to the war in sight. I must wait as its conclusion unfurls.

I am somewhat heartened by replacing my secretary of war with his chief legal adviser, Edwin M. Stanton. I have high hopes that Mr. Stanton can put the War Department aright, as it has gotten very confused of late.

I took special note of how you signed your last letter. You used only your first name. May I address you as Lettie? You may address me as A. I am a simple man. I do not believe in formal salutations among friends.

Sincerely yours,

*A. Lincoln*

A. Lincoln

To learn more about Edwin M. Stanton, visit winslowpress.com.

*Secretary of War Edwin M. Stanton*

# January 14, 1862

Dear A.,

This morning, snow covered Master Tucker's land with a lacy petticoat. I have lived on the Tucker Plantation all my days. I have seen snow only three times. To welcome the snow's rare beauty, I snapped a twig from the low-down branches of a pine bush, and wrote my name. My name sure looked fine resting in the snow's clean white softness. It made me sad to have to mash my writing away so's no one would see it after I was gone.

I would be pleased if you called me just Lettie.

Your friend,

*Lettie*

Lettie
**Tucker Plantation**
**Charleston, South Carolina**

# January 23, 1862

**Executive Mansion, Washington**

Dear Lettie,

Willie, Tad, and I enjoyed a good part of this day together. It is too cold to play on the White House grounds. We spent our morning wrestling on the expensive Oriental carpet Mrs. Lincoln purchased when we moved into the Executive Mansion nearly a year ago. These wrestling matches annoy Mrs. Lincoln, but my sons love them. Today I coaxed the boys off her rug by inviting them to my study, where I read them several of your letters.

Tad envies Elias. He wishes he had a set of blowing quills to call his own, although he is familiar with another kind of music. One day he went up to the attic in the White House and discovered the bells that alert the servants. He set the bells to clanging all at once, and the staff was thoroughly confused. My cabinet complains that our boys are spoiled, but I am pleased to see them having so much fun.

Willie has asked me to solicit your father's advice for saving the grass on the White House lawn. You see, Willie's pet goat, Lucy, tramples the lawn and snacks on the grass every chance she gets. To make matters worse, she then leaves her waste all over the place. What should be the most admired lawn in all of Washington has become a mess of mashed grass and goat droppings.

When spring returns, Willie and I will work together to restore the lawn to its right condition. But how are we to proceed? Your father must surely know.

Yours truly,

*A. Lincoln*

A. Lincoln

# February 3, 1862

Dear A.,

Here is my pap's know-how for restoring a lawn to its natural true green. For some of these, you don't even have to wait for spring.

1. Plant marigolds at the lawn's edge. Their poisonous leaves kill off hungry bugs.
2. Mix Lucy's droppings with chopped hay and horse manure to make fertilizer.
3. Spread the manure mix.
4. When the days get hot again, water the grass in the morning and at night.
5. Keep Lucy off the grass.

Yours for true,

*Lettie*

Lettie
**Tucker Plantation**
**Charleston, South Carolina**

---

*Background: The White House, with a statue of Thomas Jefferson in front, 1861*

To learn more about the Lincolns' pets, visit winslowpress.com.

45

**Executive Mansion, Washington**

Dear Lettie,

Today I celebrate my fifty-third birthday. My life has seen more than half a century. I find that birthdays are a good time to reflect. Pondering keeps a man honest with himself.

Some days I feel removed from the humble man this country elected to serve as its president. Though I care little for social niceties, I live nobly here in Washington. This is due, in part, to Mrs. Lincoln, who insists on decorum in all matters.

I prefer to wear my shirtsleeves and carpet slippers. But a waistcoat and cravat have now become my uniform. And though I enjoy sporting a stovepipe hat, it has come to be expected that I wear the hat as a symbol of my authority. (The hat is a great place to store important documents, but wearing it puts pressure on my temples. This is a deterrent to thinking clearly.)

All I ever wanted was to serve people. But it seems we equate a man's leadership abilities with the accessories that surround him.

I have made a birthday resolution. I will lead this nation with what I believe to be true in my heart, not from the hat that sits on my head.

Sincerely yours,

*A. Lincoln*

A. Lincoln

*President Abraham Lincoln in his stovepipe hat while visiting the Fifth Corps headquarters near Sharpsburg, Maryland, 1862*

# February 26, 1862

Dear A.,

I would give my eyeteeth to have a noble life. Do you ever keep my letters in your hat? This may be the closest I ever come to living in high style.

Seeing as there is no more frost on the soil, Pap and I planted my dahlia bulb. We dug a hole at the front of the quarters, where the bulb's blossom will brighten the place we call home.

Yours for true,

*Lettie*

Lettie
**Tucker Plantation**
**Charleston, South Carolina**

# March 10, 1862

Dear A.,

   Near a month has passed, and I have not heard from you. I know you are a busy man being the president, so I will not pester you. Has thinking on your high-hattin' life affected you so badly?

Yours for true,

*Lettie*

Lettie
**Tucker Plantation**
**Charleston, South Carolina**

*A slave woman by her cabin*

# April 16, 1862

Dear A.,

   Could it be that my letters are not reaching you? Have your secretaries stopped them? You know I will keep writing, no matter what.

*Lettie*

Lettie
**Tucker Plantation**
**Charleston, South Carolina**

*A photo of Lincoln that captures a melancholy expression*

# April 18, 1862

**Executive Mansion, Washington**

Dear Lettie,

It seems you sent your last letter just as I was sitting down to pen this one. I regret that you have not heard from me in so long a time. My delay in writing has only partly to do with the astute work of my secretaries. Your last two letters were indeed confiscated by White House mail officials. Thankfully, the letters were not opened. They were directed to me immediately, because they were addressed to Willie.

Lettie, I have suffered a great tragedy. Willie took his last breath of life on February 20. Willie is dead. Both he and Tad suffered wretched fevers. Tad's fever did not hang on. Tad recovered. But the heat in Willie's body sent him into a fit of delirium.

Tad is now the only child living at the White House. My poor Mary has fallen down a dark well of grief. She has taken to her bed. She will not leave home. Her anguish even prevented her from attending Willie's funeral. Robert and Tad faced the loss of their brother without their mother's guiding hand.

*(Left) Willie Lincoln. (Right) Mary Todd Lincoln in mourning*

**To learn more about children in the White House, visit winslowpress.com.**

Many nights I weep alone in my room. I have not been able to see clearly through the blur of my tears; thus I have not written to you. Please accept my apologies for the sudden break in our correspondence.

It is best that you now address your letters to Tad.

People sometimes wonder if I, as the president, ever suffer. The president is not exempt from hardships, or, as your mother has referred to them, bitter times.

For me, this is a time too bitter to name.

In sorrow,

*A. Lincoln*

A. Lincoln

# May 1, 1862

Dear A.,

What you wrote to tell me about Willie is a soul-sorry shame. But I know Willie is in Heaven. I know this because when Missy Kat learned me to read, she did it by showing me the Bible. There are readings from the Bible that always stay with me. One I remember is, "Blessed are those that mourn, for they shall be comforted."

I believe Heaven is a happy, beautiful place. When you go to your room to weep, try to imagine Willie being happy.

Willie don't need no telescope in Heaven. He can look at the stars close up.

Yours for true,

*Lettie*

Lettie
**Tucker Plantation**
**Charleston, South Carolina**

**To learn more about Lincoln's religious beliefs, visit winslowpress.com.**

*Lincoln's stepmother, Sarah Bush Johnston Lincoln, at age 77*

**Executive Mansion, Washington**

Dear Lettie,

Thank you for offering me a bit of solace. Though grief still has me in its grip, you have given me a comforting way to reflect on Willie's death. I shared your last letter with my son Tad. He, too, was consoled by your words.

The Bible is one of this world's most precious volumes. Your mention of it reminded me of an important period in my youth. I first discovered the great Good Book when I was a boy growing up in Gentryville, Indiana.

You see, my mother died when I was nine years old. My father remarried a very kind woman named Sarah Bush Johnston. I took an instant liking to my stepmother. She encouraged me to read the Bible every day. Even as a boy, I found answers to many of life's trials within its pages. Though I own a Bible here at the White House, my reading of it has fallen off considerably in recent months.

Just yesterday, though, I called Tad to my room, where we read the Bible together and relished its unsurpassed wisdom.

I'm beginning to see myself as an instrument of Providence, placed on this earth in the center of this war for God's own designs. Perhaps there is a great movement of God to end slavery, and a man would be a fool to stand in His way.

Sincerely and respectfully,

*A. Lincoln*

A. Lincoln

*May 17, 1862*

# June 4, 1862

Dear A.,

Something feels wrong way deep in my belly. Whenever this happens, I know a real bad thing is coming to pass. Mama says your insides know things before your outsides do. Last night Mama boiled me dogwood bark tea to settle my belly. But it's not a stomachache I got. What I got is a sure feeling that evil will be meeting up with me soon. When this feeling starts to press real hard, there is not enough tea in all of South Carolina to head it off.

My dahlia has started to poke its stem and leaves out from the dirt. It is a happy sight. It takes the sting off my worry.

Yours for true,

*Lettie*

Lettie
**Tucker Plantation**
**Charleston, South Carolina**

*(Left) Background: Meeting Street, near Broad Street, with St. Michael's Church in middle, Charleston, South Carolina, ca. 1865. (Right) A view of ruined buildings seen from porch of Circular Church, 150 Meeting Street, Charleston, South Carolina, at end of war, ca. 1865*

# June 30, 1862

**Executive Mansion, Washington**

Dear Lettie,

You have been blessed—and cursed—with the power of premonition. I regret that your sense of impending trouble has caused you such agitation. Perhaps you should welcome the tea your mother prepares for you. Though the tea may not stop whatever evil you feel is coming, it may calm you so that you can face it.

The war between the states rages on, and its pace quickens. Just this month, the Union lost precious ground in its

attempts to drive back the Confederate Army. In Richmond, General George McClellan's troops suffered a surprise attack by Robert E. Lee's Confederate rebels. Nearly 25,000 men were killed or wounded in the fight.

With Willie's loss still heavy in my heart, I shudder to think of the mothers, wives, sisters, and others who, as I write this letter, are crying tears for their beloved men lost in battle.

If I, like you, Lettie, was given the ability to sense adversity, perhaps I could somehow affect this war's outcome. I have not been bestowed this gift, however. So, I am left to face the pressures of war with uncertainty lurking at every turn.

Sincerely,

*A. Lincoln*

A. Lincoln

To learn more about generals of the Civil War, visit winslowpress.com.

*(Left) Camp Winfield Scott, headquarters of General George B. McClellan, near Yorktown, Virginia, May 3, 1862. (Right) President Lincoln and General George B. McClellan meeting at McClellan's headquarters, Antietam, Maryland, October 1862*

*Dear A.,*

*Mama and Pap don't never argue, though last night, when I was trying to sleep on my palette, I overheard them talking a heated streak. Mama says Pap should not fret himself with a war fighted by white men. Pap was close to hollering when he told Mama that even though this war has the face of white people on it, the souls of coloreds is at the war's core—that our very lives are at stake.*

*You ever hear of a man named Frederick Douglass? Pap said Frederick Douglass is our colored king—that he has what's good and right for Negro people always in the front of his mind. And that he, being a free colored man, can talk out loud about what is best for nigras.*

*That's when Pap mentioned you, A. Pap says you and Frederick Douglass got opposite views on this war, and on coloreds. He says you are a man of the law—a lawyer—and that even though you know deep down that slavery is wrong, you still let slavery go on. And Pap told Mama that you care more about keeping the Union together than about seeing slavery end.*

*While Mama and Pap were talking, Pap put a question to Mama. He asked her, why don't you just make us free, since you's the president and can do as you please? Mama didn't have an answer for Pap, but she did tell Pap he's been thinking too much on things that ain't in his power to do anything about.*

*When Mama and Pap was done talking, and the night got to be still, Pap's question whispered loud inside me.*

*President Lincoln, why don't you just make us free?*

*Yours for true,*

*Lettie*

Lettie
**Tucker Plantation, Charleston, South Carolina**

**To learn more about Frederick Douglass, visit winslowpress.com.**

*Frederick Douglass*

**Executive Mansion, Washington**

Dear Lettie:

It is wise to ask questions. Questions are the stepping-stones that lead to truth. I appreciate that you inquire in such a forthright manner.

Your mother and father are right about several things. Frederick Douglass speaks fervently and articulately on behalf of your people. Mr. Douglass is an ardent supporter of the abolitionist cause. Though he is one of my chief critics, I can truly say he is a remarkable man. Despite this, Frederick Douglass and I suffer our differences.

As a lawyer, I have, for hours on end, pondered the institution of slavery. I have referred to the Declaration of Independence many times, hoping its wisdom will point out an answer to the baffling question of where a colored man's plight fits into the notion that all men are created equal. Though I believe it is wrong to own a man, woman, or child as one would own an object such as a kettle or a hoof pick, I also believe that ending slavery is not as simple as Frederick Douglass and many other abolitionists make it out to be.

Sometimes I think the best solution would be colonization, since colored people, even if emancipated, would have little chance of ever achieving equality with so many ignorant whites about. Your people would have better opportunities in other lands, such as Liberia or Haiti.

Indeed, I do care deeply about preserving the Union. The sooner the national authority can be restored, the closer the Union will be to its fomer condition. This cannot be, however, until several rebel states that have seceded from the Union—your very own South Carolina among them— agree to return.

What's more, the slaveholding border states—Kentucky, Missouri, Maryland, and Delaware—have refused to join the

**To learn more about the abolitionist movement, visit winslowpress.com.**

*A slave family, 1862*

Confederacy. If I were to put an immediate stop to slavery, it is quite likely these states would ally themselves with the South right away. While I am willing to consider a policy of emancipation for your people, I also worry that it would incense the slave owners in the Confederacy, and all hope of preserving the Union would be permanently destroyed. I am loathe to undertake such a risk at this time.

Aside from considering the state of the Union, perhaps most relevant to the issue of slavery is the Constitution. The fact is this: under our Constitution, the federal government has no power to abolish slavery in states where it currently exists. As president, I cannot, in good conscience, abolish slavery without violating the very Constitution I have sworn to protect.

I am at a troubling fork in the road, Lettie.

Very truly yours,

*A. Lincoln*

A. Lincoln

# August 5, 1862

Dear A.,

I learned a new word from reading your last letter. The word is "inquire." From now on, I will not ask. I will inquire. A., I want to inquire why you make things so convoluted when they don't have to be.

If you believe slavery is wrong, why are you wasting time thinking so much about rebel states and border states?

I am beginning to think that Frederick Douglass is right in saying that you couldn't care less about Negroes.

If you believe slavery is wrong, why don't you just make things right?

Yours for true,

*Lettie*

Lettie

P.S. My dahlia has bloomed! Its flower is a burst of yellow that is my own little piece of sunshine.

To learn more about Northern, border and rebel states, visit winslowpress.com.

*Slaves picking cotton while white overseer checks on their work.*

# August 16, 1862

**Executive Mansion, Washington**

Dear Lettie:

As I write to you this day, I am seated in my favorite chair, in my private quarters, in a place I have come to call by its Latin name—my *sanctum sanctorum*—my sacred room. My Bible lies open in my lap. I have been consulting the Bible's pages each morning. It seems I am drawn to the Bible more and more these days. Similarly, I have been drawn to reading your latest letters many times over. Lettie, your agitation is quite clear, and your questions—your inquiries—have given me great pause.

During a recent trip to Virginia, I met a woman named Abigail Briggs, who urged me to make provisions that would have her husband released from prison. Abigail told me that she and her husband were devout Christians; thus, her husband had no business in jail. Also, Abigail spoke of her difficulty in maintaining her plantation and her slaves without her husband. I asked Abigail how it is that she can consider herself a Christian, yet still own slaves. Abigail was stunned by my inquiry. She had no answer.

I later realized that I suffer the same contradiction. I consider myself of Christian belief, yet slavery continues under my leadership as president.

If I could save the Union without freeing any slave, I would. But at the same time, if I could only save the Union by freeing all slaves, I would do that too.

It seems that I am imprisoned in an eternal paradox.

Most sincerely yours,

*A. Lincoln*

A. Lincoln

*A print based on a fanciful painting of Lincoln by David Gilmour Blythe*

Dear A.,

You are between what Pap calls a rock and a hard place. In thinking about you this way, I guess I'm stuck in my own paradox. I'm sorry that all of this is so bothersome to you, but at the same time, I'm glad for it, because it's got you thinking deep on slavery.

Two men keep coming here to have long meetings with Master Tucker in his study. Twice before they been here. Today made it three times. Master Tucker and them two men were holed up in that study from till after breakfast to way past the middle of the day.

When the afternoon started to slip toward dusk, Mama told me to take the men a platter she had prepared with salted fish, corn cakes, and brandied peaches. When I eased open the study door, the two men were seated across from Master Tucker, leaning in hard and frowning. Not one of the men took notice of me. The three of them kept up with their meeting as if I was no more than dust showing up on a sunbeam. I set down the tray, wiped both my hands on my shift, and went to leave.

Then something strange happened as I was closing the study door behind me. I heard Master Tucker say, "Okay then, Roy is the one."

Roy is my pap's name.

What does Pap have do with those two frowning men? I'm scared Pap's in some kind of trouble.

I will inquire with Pap himself.

*Lettie*

Lettie
**Tucker Plantation, Charleston, South Carolina**

---

*(Left) Young slave woman. (Right) Plantation slave quarters, Port Royal Island, S.C.*

To learn more about southern cooking, visit winslowpress.com.

# September 2, 1862

**Executive Mansion, Washington**

Dear Lettie,

Weariness has overtaken me, yet I spend many nights awake, unable to sleep. The war has become a never-ending nightmare. I pen this letter in the night's waning hours as the heat of Washington hangs heavy above me. Writing makes use of my wakefulness.

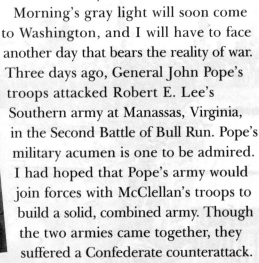

Morning's gray light will soon come to Washington, and I will have to face another day that bears the reality of war. Three days ago, General John Pope's troops attacked Robert E. Lee's Southern army at Manassas, Virginia, in the Second Battle of Bull Run. Pope's military acumen is one to be admired. I had hoped that Pope's army would join forces with McClellan's troops to build a solid, combined army. Though the two armies came together, they suffered a Confederate counterattack. Lee's men swept Union forces from the field. Yesterday, the beaten Northern troops plodded into Washington.

Lettie, there is little hope of the war's end. If the Union is to survive, the North must have a battlefield victory. If I am to take measures to ameliorate the condition of slavery, the Union must be in a condition of strength. For now, I can only pray that a Union triumph is near.

Sincerely,

*A. Lincoln*

A. Lincoln

---

*(Left) General John Pope. (Right) Federal artillery park, Yorktown, Virginia. Background: Federal artillery park, Yorktown, Virginia*

**To learn more about generals of the Civil War, visit winslowpress.com.**

Dear A.,

Seems we both got good reason to be weary. I can hardly hold my pen to write this letter. I am tired, and my fingers ache. September has done this to me. I hate September. September brings on a load of work we have to do to get ready for winter.

Come autumn, me and my ma stock Master Tucker's larder, putting food away for when December's here, when not much on the Almighty's earth has a mind for growing. Our days are filled with peeling bushels of apples to dry, washing crocks for storing peaches, and stringing up long ropes of beans that we'll cook in fatback when the cold sets in.

For Pap, the harvest season is double-time hard work. Soon as the cock crows, Pap sets to priming and stalk-cutting tobacco. Master Tucker calls Pap his tobacco man, seeing as Pap knows the best and fastest way to pick the tobacco leaves when they turn ripe.

At night, Pap gets very quiet. Mama says the harvest time squeezes the sap from Pap's veins. Tonight I told Pap about the two men in Master Tucker's study, and I told him what they said about him being the one. When I asked Pap what they meant, Pap didn't answer. His jaw got tight. He would not look in my direction. I know Pap's tired from all the harvest work, but it ain't like him to not speak to me.

When I asked Pap a second time about what I heard in the master's study, he told me I should not be puttin' my ears in other people's business. To my way of thinking, anything having to do with my very own pa is my business for true. But still the knot in my belly is telling me Pap's got bad times ahead.

*Lettie*

Lettie

**Tucker Plantation, Charleston,
South Carolina**

To learn more about tobacco,
visit winslowpress.com.

To learn more about the
major battles of the Civil War,
visit winslowpress.com.

# September 11, 1862

**Executive Mansion, Washington**

Dear Lettie,

In the same way that your father primes tobacco leaf by leaf, I thought I could remove slavery in bits. But as time passes, as the war continues to eat its way through our land, I see this is not so.

When I was a boy, one of my chores was to bust wood with an iron wedge and a mallet. I remember how the wedge would split the wood with its sharp iron tooth. I think of those chore days often now.

Slavery is a wedge that has driven our nation apart. It has divided us with a sure force. Four years ago, when I ran for the Senate, I spoke this belief at the Republican convention in Springfield, Illinois. I told my listeners that a house divided against itself cannot stand.

Though it appears to many that I have not taken definitive action on slavery, I have never lost sight of my conviction to restore national unity.

I have come to an important decision. If our nation is to be whole again, I cannot address slavery in any small measure. I must strike a piercing blow against slavery lest we remain a nation asunder. I cannot do this, however, until the time is right.

In matters of great magnitude, prudence and patience are the keys to right action. I will exercise these virtues until I am moved to act.

Very truly yours,

*A. Lincoln*

A. Lincoln

To read Lincoln's speech at the 1858 Republican Convention, visit winslowpress.com.

*Confederate fortifications, with cannon, Yorktown, Virginia, June, 1862. Background: Howitzer gun captured by Butterfield's Brigade near Hanover Courthouse, May 27, 1862*

# September 17, 1862

Dear A.,

As Mama would say, you are on the road to right thinking. I wish I could get to thinking rightly about Elias. Even though he is my brother, I sometimes wish he'd turn into a toad, and go live in a patch of high grass.

Elias has taken to whistling at his quills all day long, so's he'll be ready to play them for our Ring Shout harvest dance. In October, at the end of the harvest season, all us slaves here at Tucker's place will gather up, make a circle, and stomp a dance to praise Heaven for another good crop.

This year, Elias wants to get the dancing started with his quills. But if the truth be told, Elias's quill playing hasn't got any better since last Christmas. He still makes nothing but noise with them quills.

I am not a sickly girl, and I don't suffer much from body ailments. But when Elias gets going on his quills, my whole head aches. I cannot dance the Ring Shout with a pain in my head.

Pap says that to the ears of the Almighty, Elias's quill playing is sweet, good music.

I wish I had the Almighty's ears.

*Lettie*

Lettie
**Tucker Plantation**
**Charleston, South Carolina**

*(Left) Several generations of a slave family, J. J. Smith's Plantation, Beaufort, South Carolina, 1862. (Right) A slave boy about the same age as Elias*

To learn more about slave music, visit winslowpress.com.

75

# September 25, 1862

**Executive Mansion, Washington**

Dear Lettie,

Eight days ago, McClellan's Union forces launched a series of attacks on Lee's Southern troops at Sharpsburg, a town on Antietam Creek in Maryland. McClellan's men forced Lee's army to retreat to Virginia.

The Battle of Antietam marked the bloodiest day of the war to date. Thousands of men from both sides died. Thousands more were wounded. While I am sorry for the tremendous casualties suffered, I cannot help but feel a sense of gratitude for the North's success. It is an indication of Divine will that God is in favor of abolishing slavery.

This victory has opened a door for me. A door that will, ultimately, swing open for you and your family.

Three days ago I assembled my cabinet and read to them a draft of a document I have named the Emancipation Proclamation. This decree will call for the freedom of all slaves living in the Confederacy. My proclamation is not yet absolute. But if the rebel states that have seceded from the Union do not return to the Union by January 1, I will make the Emancipation Proclamation official.

News of this draft proclamation has already begun to spread. I am certain you will soon hear all kinds of speculation and debate about it.

Most sincerely,

*A. Lincoln*

A. Lincoln

---

To learn more about the major battles of the Civil War, visit winslowpress.com.

*Antietam battlefield on the day of the battle, photo by Matthew B. Brady, September 1862*

# October 8, 1862

Dear A.,

I read your letter with a joy too full to name. You are right. Word of your proclamation has come right here to the Tucker Plantation! The rumors and hearsay are flying around so fast, they're near to burning the wind.

Yesterday we danced our Ring Shout. This year's harvest dance circle was a double celebration. We danced happy for corn, happy for tobacco and wheat. And we stomped with true gladness for the promise of freedom.

I danced my own bit of thankfulness for my dahlia flower, which is starting to wither. Even though I will dig up its bulb and tuck it back in its croaker sack at the end of this month, I am grateful for the gift of its beauty.

Yours in gratitude,

*Lettie*

Lettie
**Tucker Plantation**
**Charleston, South Carolina**

P.S. Elias's quills never sounded so good.

**Executive Mansion, Washington**

Dear Lettie:

I am glad to have given you cause to rejoice. These are such distressing times. Every bit of celebration is to be savored. Though our nation is in a cauldron of change, I am filled with renewed hope.

Yours truly,

*A. Lincoln*

A. Lincoln

October 20, 1862

*Confederate fortifications, with cannon, Yorktown, Virginia, June 1862*

# November 2, 1862

Dear A.,

Those same two men who came to Master Tucker's study last summer visited again today. Right quick, I asked Mama if I could serve them victuals, so's I could hear what they was saying. Even though they didn't even take notice of me, I was listening hard on them.

Just like before, they spoke of Pap. Master Tucker told them all about Pap's knowin' of trees, and soil, and tobacco, and beans. And he said he was glad that Pap had been here for another harvest season. Those two men seemed to be baited to Master Tucker's praises of Pap. They was all ears. One of the men said now that the harvest time is done, he and Master Tucker could get down to business.

Then all three men started talking about you, A. They was saying you are full of bluff. They said your draft proclamation ain't worth the paper it is written on, and that your plan to free the slaves is a bunch of pig slop.

I figured the best way to find out what's for true is to inquire with you myself. Is your plan for true? Or is your Emancipation Proclamation nothing more than hogwash?

*Lettie*

Lettie
**Tucker Plantation**
**Charleston, South Carolina**

To learn more about
the election of 1862,
visit winslowpress.com.

# November 11, 1862

**Executive Mansion, Washington**

Dear Lettie,

When a man takes a bold stance, it makes him a convenient target for ridicule. It does not surprise me that my proclamation has come under such scrutiny, and that you are hearing such harsh things about it. The recent elections were a Republican disaster, and I have never felt so much alone.

You can be assured, however, that I am steadfast in my course of action.

Most truly yours,

A. Lincoln

*Abraham Lincoln wearing his cravat and waistcoat*

Dear A.,

It is hard to believe that you, of all people, can ever feel alone. I now feel alone in many ways too.

Once, when I was a little girl, a diamond-backed snake took me by surprise and bit me bad. Since then, I have believed that pain hurts worse when it comes up on you without no warning, and when no one else is nearby to comfort you when it happens.

A., I got pain that's more bad than ten snake bites. Even though I've had an inkling that trouble was around the corner, an awful thing has come at me that feels as though it's come out of the clear blue. Pap's been sold, A.! Master Tucker has gone back on his promise to Missy Kat. He said one thing but did another. He lied.

It happened three days back. With not even a hint, it happened. Elias and me were working alongside Mama in the anteroom next to the scullery. We were stitching garlands to decorate the balusters for the holiday season soon to be coming. All a sudden, we heard a commotion outside. Missy Kat was hollering, telling her daddy to stop. When Mama, Elias, and me came running, we saw Pap roped up in the back of a wagon with two men in front on the drive-seat. It was the two men from Master Tucker's study.

Pap was tied at his hands and feet. Pap was gritting his teeth. There was tears in Pap's eyes. My own pa was crying! Master Tucker was telling Missy Kat to go back inside. He was saying that the war has put him heavy in debt, and that Pap would fetch the best price at auction. He said Pap would bring two hundred fifty dollars. And he was telling Missy Kat that his promise was made in more prosperous times, when there wasn't no war, when he didn't owe money.

Soon Mama got to screaming, then me. And Elias was calling out Pap's name. With all her might, Mama was asking Master Tucker to please not take our Pap. Master Tucker told Mama there was no other way. He told us we could come to the wharf to see Pap at auction, and that if nobody bought Pap, Pap could come home.

That auction put a chill to my bones, A. One girl who looked not much older than me was forced to stand on the auction block with her bare naked breasts showing, so's the menfolk who was doing the bidding could see if the girl would make a good nursing mammy.

When they put Pap on the block, Pap looked straight ahead. He hardly blinked. And Pap didn't flinch when the auction man pulled back his lips so's everybody could see how strong his teeth was. That's when both me and Elias buried our faces in Mama's skirts. Even though I wasn't lookin', I heard the auction man call Pap the same thing Master Tucker had once called him—a commodity.

Pap was bought up right quick. He fetched three hundred dollars from a Louisiana master. When Pap was sold, his new master took him in a hurry. Pap is now where Mama had been before she came to Tucker's. Pap is in cotton country, where one master is as mean as ten.

Mama, Elias, and me rode back to the Tucker Plantation on the flatbed of Master's Tucker's wagon, with Master Tucker and Missy Kat up front.

Since then, Missy Kat won't speak to her pa. Since then, Mama has gone quiet, too. At night, I hear her weeping in the dark. In the day, she looks lost. Elias now sleeps with Pap's work shirt. Me, I'm feeling like a bird in a box—fidgety, mad, wantin' to break loose.

*Lettie*

Lettie

P.S. Today I dug up the bulb left from last summer's dahlia bloom. I tucked the bulb away in an old kerchief. It is all I have of my pa.

To learn more about the slave trade, visit winslowpress.com.

*A slave auction from an original sketch by Theodore R. Davis*

83

# December 4, 1862

**Executive Mansion, Washington**

Dear Lettie,

Your letter struck sorrow in my heart. Unforeseen loss is perhaps the worst loss of all. When Willie was taken from me and Mrs. Lincoln so suddenly, it was as though I had fallen down a great precipice. The unexpected loss of a beloved one is now common between us, Lettie. But I have found that when mourning is shared with one who understands, the mourning lessens.

On the first day of this month, I delivered my annual message to Congress. I asked my listeners for support of my program of emancipation. I said: "In giving freedom to the slave, we assure freedom to the free. . . ."

I approach the coming New Year with great hope for slavery's end.

I implore you, too, to have faith.

Yours sincerely,

*A. Lincoln*

A. Lincoln

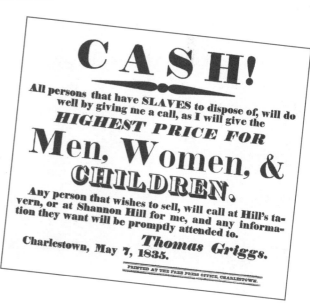

*(Left) "Auction & Negro Sales," Whitehall Street, Atlanta, Georgia.*
*(Right) Advertising for purchase of slaves by Thomas Griggs,*
*Charlestown, May 7, 1835*

# December 13, 1862

Dear A.,

I do not want to make slight of Willie's death. But I feel our loss is not a common one. You lost Willie to natural causes. I lost Pap in a way that is truly unnatural. Fever took Willie from you. Cruelty took my Pap. Willie is in Heaven. Pap is in Hell come to Earth.

That bees' nest of questions is back at me. So, I will inquire with you here, A.

How is it that my Pap can be here with me one day, loving me, showing me how to make a bulb turn to a flower, then be gone from me in a sudden? How is it that one man call sell off another? How is it, A.? How can this be?

I am so sad. I don't know no answers.

Mama says it is not right to beg in the sight of the Almighty. But I am *begging*, A. Please make your emancipation come true. Please end slavery.

*Lettie*

Lettie

*A page from* The Liberty Almanac, *1847*

SERVANT WOMAN FOR SALE.—We have for private sale a very valuable servant woman, a good cook, washer, &c.   Apply to R. W. DYER & Co.

In the same paper, July 20, 1846, Mr. Green advertises as follows:—

SALE OF HOUSEHOLD AND KITCHEN FURNITURE.—On Thursday, the 30th instant, at 10 o'clock, A.M., will be sold, at the auction rooms of the subscriber, a genteel lot of Furniture, worthy the attention of housekeepers, as the sale must positively take place.

Terms of sale: All sums of, and under, $20, cash; over $20, a credit of 60 and 90 days, for notes satisfactorily endorsed, bearing interest.

A. GREEN, Auctioneer.

UPON THE SAME DAY, AT 5 O'CLOCK, P. M., AND AT THE SAME PLACE, WILL BE sold a very likely and valuable servant Boy, about 17 years of age, a slave for life.

Terms of sale: One half cash, and the balance in 60 days, to be secured by note satisfactorily endorsed, bearing interest.

july 20—2taw1w&3taw1w A. GREEN, Auctioneer.

For some reason the sale did not come off on the 30th, and accordingly the Intelligencer of July 31st, contains the following:—

SERVANT AT AUCTION.—The sale of the servant boy, advertised to take place at my store on Thursday, the 30th instant., is postponed until Thursday, the 6th of August, at 5 o'clock, P. M., when the sale will positively take place at my auction store.

july 31---eod A. GREEN, Auctioneer.

---

### Shame of the National Man-Trade.

In 1802, the Grand Jury of Alexandria said—" These dealers, in the persons of our fellow-men, collect within this District, from various parts, numbers of these victims of slavery, and lodge them in some place of confinement until they have completed their numbers. They are then turned out into our streets, and exposed to view *loaded with chains.*"

In 1816, Judge Morrell, charging the Grand Jury of Washington, said—" The frequency with which the streets of the city had been *crowded with manacled captives,* sometimes on the Sabbath, could not fail to shock the feelings of all humane persons."

June 22, 1827, the Alexandria Gazette said:—" Scarcely a week passes without some of these wretched creatures being driven through our streets. After having been confined, and sometimes manacled in a loathsome prison, they are turned out in public view to take their departure for the South. The children and some of the women are generally crowded into a cart or wagon, while others follow on foot, not unfrequently *handcuffed and chained together.*

In 1829, the Grand Jury of Washington said:—" The manner in which they (slaves) are brought and confined in these places, *and carried through our streets,* is necessarily such as to excite the most painful feelings."

In 1830, the Washington Spectator said:—" Let it be known to the citizens of America, that at the very time when the procession, which contained the President of the United States and his cabinet, was marching in triumph to the Capitol, another kind of procession was marching another way; and that consisted of colored human beings, *handcuffed in pairs,* and driven along by what had the appearance of a man on horseback! A similar scene was repeated on Saturday last; a drove consisting of males and females, *chained in couples,* starting from Roby's tavern on foot for Alexandria, where, with others, they are to embark on board a slave-ship in waiting to convey them to the South."

---

### Horrors of the National Man-Trade.

The Alexandria Gazette, as quoted above, adds:—" Here you may behold fathers and brothers leaving behind them the dearest objects of affection, and moving slowly along in the mute agony of despair—there the young mother sobbing over the infant whose innocent smiles seem but to increase her misery.

# December 20, 1862

**Executive Mansion, Washington**

Dear Lettie,

Perhaps it is absurd of me to compare Willie's death to the sale of your father. But ever since Willie died, I have been haunted with similar questions to those you ask yourself. How, I wonder, could my son be taken from me at such a young age? Why is it that Tad survived his fever, when Willie succumbed? When will I know peace from this tragedy?

I wish I had answers to your inquiries, and to my own, but I do not. The natural law of things is not for me or you to decide. However, as president, it is within my power to impact the laws that govern our nation. And I will.

Humbly and respectfully,

*A. Lincoln*

A. Lincoln

*Thomas "Tad" Lincoln dressed in his colonel's uniform at about age 8*

*Dear A.,*

   *Pap once told me a promise is not a promise until it is kept. Master Tucker made a promise to Missy Kat, and he went back on it. I will never again let myself believe in a promise until it comes true.*

   *For now, I can only take your words as intentions.*

*Lettie*

Lettie

# January 1, 1863

**Executive Mansion, Washington**
**The evening hour**
Dear Lettie,

By the time this letter reaches you, you will know of your freedom. I woke early today after a fitful night's sleep. As a cold white morning rose over Washington—and a new year dawned on the world—I put the finishing touches on my Emancipation Proclamation.

From this day forward, all persons held as slaves shall be forever free.

Lettie Tucker, you can consider slavery a part of your past. Today I bestow on you your birthright—freedom.

Our traditional New Year's Day reception was held in the White House just hours after I finished the proclamation. The gathering was the first official one at which Mrs. Lincoln has appeared since Willie's death. There was little festivity on Mrs. Lincoln's part. Though she wore garlands in her hair, a black mourning shawl shrouded her head.

Once the reception was fully underway, I retired to my office with several members of my cabinet and other officials for the formal signing of the proclamation. I have awaited this day for a long time. My hand trembled as I signed my name with a gold pen. As you know, I customarily sign my documents "A. Lincoln." But today I spelled out my name in its entirety. As my signature marked the page, I told my cabinet that if my name ever goes into history, it will be for this act.

*The first reading of the Emancipation Proclamation by Lincoln to his cabinet.*

To end this first day of 1863, I returned to my desk to pen you this letter.

My hands are still trembling, but I am calm.

Most truly yours,

*Abraham Lincoln*

Abraham Lincoln

From left to right: Edwin M. Stanton (secretary of war), Salmon P. Chase (secretary of the Treasury), Lincoln, Gideon Welles (secretary of the navy), William H. Seward (secretary of state), Caleb B. Smith (secretary of the Interior), Montgomery Blair (postmaster general) and Edward Bates (attorney general), engraving by Alexander Hay Ritchie after F. B. Carpenter

# January 9, 1863

Dear A.,

It would not surprise me if the ink on your letter soon smears off the page. I have read your letter near to a hundred times and have traced the word "free" with my finger twice as many times as that.

Master Tucker is the one who told us about your official Emancipation Proclamation. Mama and me were boiling up a batch of hominy when we heard the smokehouse bell coming from the far fields. The only time that bell rings is when something can't wait.

At the smokehouse, it was Master Tucker who was ringing the bell. He looked tired and filled with hurt. Missy Kat was standing next to Master Tucker, who told us the news simply and quietly. As her pa spoke, Missy's eyes jumped from Elias to Mama, then landed square on me.

When Master Tucker was telling us of our freedom, he had pain in his voice. But Missy Kat, she was working hard to hold back from smiling.

That night at the quarters it seemed the celebrating would never end. The dancing and stomping and hoots and hollers were enough to wake the moon.

But there was something in me that could not get fully happy. In the middle of our rejoicing, I was missing Pap. All's I wanted— maybe even more than freedom itself—was to be with my daddy. Even though that party was full with joy, all's I could see was the empty spaces—the spaces where Pap wasn't.

With Pap gone, freedom is like lemonade. It is sweet and sour at the same time.

Lettie

---

**To learn more about the Emancipation Proclamation, visit winslowpress.com.**

*A print by Thomas Nast depicting a bright future for freed slaves after the Emancipation Proclamation*

# January 23, 1863

**Executive Mansion, Washington**

Dear Lettie,

It is no wonder you feel so conflicted about freedom. I have enjoyed tremendous praise for my Emancipation Proclamation, while at the same time I have suffered the slings of those who are infuriated by my decree. Such vast and contradictory reactions are vexing to the soul. However, I hold fast to the belief that dust can only settle after it has been stirred.

*A. Lincoln*

A. Lincoln

Dear A.,

The Tucker Plantation is now a strange sight. Used to be, you could look out over Master Tucker's land and see black bodies bent with workin'. But soon after freedom came, most all the nigras livin' here packed their croaker sacks and headed off to find a new life. Folks as old as the wind, babies bundled tight, and everybody in between gathered themselves and left. As they went, it looked to me like some kind of slow parade moving down the lane that trails off from Tucker's land. The freedom parade, I called it.

Colored people don't have much, but those who went took everything they owned—oxen, castor oil, fire flint, broom straw, sawdust pillows, feedsack nighties, live chickens. Every last thing.

Mama, Elias, and me, we're still here. Mama, she ain't going nowhere. She says the Almighty meant us to grow where we're planted. And, she says there ain't nothin' this world has that she can't get here at Tucker's. When I reminded Mama that Pap's somewhere in this world, she got real quiet. She hasn't spoken on freedom since then. Sometimes I wonder if she truly knows she's free. She still wakes before the sun. Still goes to Master Tucker's kitchen before the cock crows. Still cooks. Still cleans. Still shells peas with her stumpy fingertips. Master Tucker has told Mama to take us and go. Says he can't afford to pay her for her work. But Mama keeps on like nothing's changed.

I love my ma, A. But I can't watch her living like a slave. I may be planted here, but I sure ain't planning on growing here. Mama and Elias don't know it yet, but come spring, I'm fixing to make my own freedom parade. I'm going to find my pap.

Yours for true,

*Lettie*

Lettie

**To learn more about life in the South after the Emancipation Proclamation, visit winslowpress.com.**

*(Left) "Colored" soldiers resting near the Aiken house, Aiken's Landing, Virginia. (Right) A detail of freed slaves in Newbern, North Carolina, wood engraving, Harper's Weekly, February 21, 1863*

# March 9, 1863

**Executive Mansion, Washington**

Dear Lettie,

I know you miss your father, and I know you are eager to venture forth. But please consider all factors. The end of slavery has brought bedlam to the Confederacy. Plantations that were once prosperous now suffer from the loss of slave labor. For many who were firm believers in slavery, the Emancipation Proclamation has fueled their hatred of colored men.

Your people are, in some respects, more vulnerable to the irrational anger of the Secesh, the men and women who loved the South as it was before freedom.

You are a child, Lettie. You risk unspeakable dangers by striking out on your own. Remember, too, your mother and brother. Surely, in this period of great upheaval, they need you now more than ever. Think not only of yourself. Stay put for now.

Sincerely,

*A. Lincoln*

A. Lincoln

# *March 30, 1863*

*Dear A.,*

*Since the day I was birthed into this world, I have been made to stay put. I have never once stepped beyond the bounds of Charleston. And whenever I left Tucker's property, I did it with a pass from my mistress.*

*You have granted us freedom. You have given every colored soul in these here Confederate states the God-given right to roam.*

*Doorknobs and fence posts are meant to stay put. But now that I, Lettie Tucker, am officially free, I will be hard-pressed to stay anyplace I don't want to be.*

*Lately, as I try to sleep, I have been looking out into the dark. Come near to a fortnight, the moon will begin to wax. Seven days before Easter Sunday, the moon will be full. I will use the moon's light to find my way to Pap.*

*If you'd wanted me to stay put, A., you should not have signed your name to your freedom paper. But you did sign your name. Your full name. I take this to mean that I am to be fully free. You put a hurtin' on my dignity by suggesting otherwise.*

*Lettie*

*Lettie*

# April 11, 1863

**Executive Mansion, Washington**

Dear Lettie,

Viewing the sky with my telescope was once a great source of pleasure. But now, as I watch the moon grow full, I worry about you.

I looked back over several of your letters and found the one dated December 13, 1862, in which you wrote of your mother's belief that we are not to beg before God. With all due respect, I disagree with your mother. I see very little difference between begging and speaking an earnest prayer.

Thus, I pray that only good comes to you.

In the time that you and I have become acquainted through these letters, I have come to see that it is futile to try and dissuade you on any matter for which you possess a strong conviction. You are a determined girl, Lettie. I have always admired that about you. Thus, I leave you with your dignity, and I wish you Godspeed.

Most truly,

*A. Lincoln*

A. Lincoln

*A photograph of Abraham Lincoln, probably by Matthew B. Brady*

Dear A.,

Two days back, I rolled me an ash cake and a hunk of salt pork in a patch of muslin. I packed up my dahlia bulb for good luck, and crept out in the night, away from Tucker's. Mama and Elias had long since been asleep when I set off. It was so deep into the night that not even the crickets had a chirp of wakefulness left. I walked away under the full moon, as I had planned. That moon was a ball of buttermilk in the black spring sky.

At first, the only sound was my breath, working hard in my chest. But when I was not even halfway down the lane that leads away from Tucker's, I heard leaves and twigs rustling toward the stone wall that meets the lane. I kept on moving, but I was scared for true.

Then came the sound of footsteps mixing in with the leaves. Soon the noise was coming closer and faster, and I couldn't help but think of Mama. I kept wondering if this was Armageddon. If the world was ending, with the full moon as its witness. That's when I heard a hooty owl calling from the trees. I knew then—this had to be the end. A hooty owl piping up beneath a full moon is a sure sign of sudden change. With fright charging up in me, I huddled close to the wall, wishing I could turn myself into one of the stones that keeps the wall standing. Then, suddenly, I heard someone calling out to me quietly.

It was Pap, A.! Pap had come back to Tucker's! And I was there to greet him.

The world did not end for me that night. Right then, the world became a whole new place. I was hugging my pap. My pap was free. Free as the moon that lit our way back to Elias and Mama.

Glory be to the Almighty!

*Lettie*

Lettie

# May 21, 1863

**Executive Mansion, Washington**

Dear Lettie,

I will cherish your last letter. It is tangible evidence that prayers are answered.

One of the members of my cabinet once told me that God is an acronym that stands for Good Orderly Direction.

Certainly, G-O-D was bestowed upon your father. I take great happiness knowing that you were the first beneficiary of this gift.

Yours sincerely,

A. Lincoln

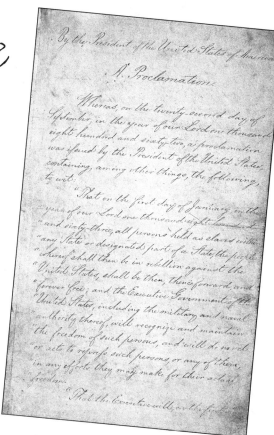

Dear A.,

You have not heard from me for a time because I have been on a journey. I am no longer at Tucker's. I am not even in South Carolina anymore. I now live in Philadelphia, Pennsylvania, a fine city where the streets are stone and where pigeons rest on rooftops. High-toned nigras are everywhere in Philadelphia. There are colored people who run their own rooming houses, printing presses, and tanneries. I even met a nigra woman who makes wigs.

I am enrolled in Miss Ellery Mayfield's School for Colored Young Ladies, where we study letters, numbers, and the domestic arts. The school is run by two white women, Ellery Mayfield and her sister Belinda. The very first lesson I learned from my teachers is that each and every one of us enrolled in the Mayfield school should consider ourselves a lady, and we should behave in a ladylike fashion. So, A., I write to you now as the fine lady you once presumed I was. I do all my writing seated at a table. And, as you can see, I now seal my letters with a wax stamp.

Pap works at the Harding lumberyard, where he hauls and stacks wood. Mama is a maid at the Rittenhouse Inn. She still wakes before the sun to meet her work, but now Mama gets paid to be a maid. On Sundays, Elias attends the Mother Bethel African Methodist Episcopal School, where he has begun to learn his letters.

Soon as we got here, Pap and I planted my dahlia bulb. Pap told me it was much too late in the season to plant the bulb. He said we'd only be able to enjoy the beginnings of its flower before its season ended.

This doesn't bother me none. To my way of thinking, we are all just beginning, and we have many flowering seasons ahead.

Yours for true,

*Lettie*

Lettie

*July 28, 1863*

A sewing class, The Freedman's Union Industrial School, engraving in "Frank Leslie's Illustrated Newspaper," September 22, 1866

To learn more about African Americans in Philadelphia in the 1800s, visit winslowpress.com.

103

# Abraham Lincoln: Historical Notes

Born on Nolin Creek near Hogenville, Kentucky, on February 12. Moves to a farm on Knob Creek, also near Hodgenville. Moves to Indiana, settling in Little Pigeon Creek, near Gentryville.

Abraham's mother, Nancy, dies of milk sickness on October 5.

Lincoln's father, Thomas Lincoln, marries Sarah Bush Johnston on December 2nd.

Abraham's sister Sarah dies in childbirth on January 28. Lincoln transports a flatboat down the Mississippi River to New Orleans.

# The Young Abraham Lincoln

Five months before Lincoln was nominated by the Republican Party to run for president, he wrote a sketch of his life, in which he described his childhood as follows:

I was born Feb. 12, 1809, in Hardin County, Kentucky. My parents were both born in Virginia, of undistinguished families—second families, perhaps, I should say. My mother, who died in my tenth year, was of a family of the name of Hanks. . . . My father . . . removed from Kentucky to . . . Indiana, in my eighth year. . . . It was a wild region, with many bears and other wild animals still in the woods. There I grew up. Of course, when I came of age, I did not know much. Still, somehow, I could read, write, and cipher . . . but that was all."

Lincoln's father, Thomas, was a hardworking carpenter and farmer who enjoyed telling tall tales to his neighbors. His mother, Nancy Hanks, by contrast was quiet and not fun loving like her husband. She could neither read nor write but quoted the Bible and recited prayers to Abraham and Sarah, Lincoln's older sister by two years. Both parents were members of the Baptist church, but because of their strong antislavery views, which were not shared by others in the congregation, they broke away with a group of like-minded thinkers and established a new church. They followed strictly the teachings of the Bible and argued against human bondage of any kind, including slavery. They also believed that God had a plan for each individual that could not be changed: what would be would be, no matter what one tried to do about it.

Besides an older sister, Lincoln had a little brother named Thomas who died shortly after he was born.

Lincoln described his childhood as "the short and simple annals of the poor." The log cabin on Nolin Creek, Kentucky, where he started his life, was small and cramped. Two years later, the Lincolns moved to a one-room cabin on Knob Creek, near Hodgenville, Kentucky. Lincoln and Sarah performed endless chores on the farm and could only attend school during the winter months, when farm life was less demanding. At the ages of seven and nine, the children moved with their parents across the Ohio River to Indiana and settled in the Little Pigeon Creek community, six miles northwest of Troy. Soon they were joined by three members of the Hanks family—Nancy's sister Elizabeth and her husband, Thomas Sparrow, as well as Dennis, a nineteen-year-old son of another sister.

A year after the family had settled in Indiana, Nancy died during an epidemic of milk sickness, caused by drinking milk from cows grazing on poisonous white snakeroot. Elizabeth and Thomas Sparrow died also, as did many others in the community. Dennis Hanks moved into the Lincoln household and shared the sleeping loft with Abraham. Although they were ten years apart in age, they became good friends.

In 1819, Thomas Lincoln remarried, this time to a widow from Elizabethtown, Kentucky, named Sarah Bush Johnston.

| 1833 | 1834 | 1837 |
|------|------|------|
| Lincoln becomes postmaster of New Salem on May 7. Is also appointed assistant surveyor in the northwest part of Sangamon County. | Runs a second time for the Illinois State Legislature and gets elected. Takes up the study of law. Is reelected to the Illinois House of Representatives. Is licensed to practice law on September 9. | Gets admitted to the Illinois Bar on March 1 and moves to Springfield on April 15. Becomes a law partner of John T. Stuart. |

She had three children by an earlier marriage. Sarah raised Abraham and his sister as if they were her own children. They were very fond of her, and years later, a few months after Lincoln was elected president, he paid her a visit. They held hands affectionately and recalled the happy times they had shared during Lincoln's early years.

Although Lincoln never had more than about a year of schooling, he was a hungry learner. Books were rare in the rural area where he grew up, but he borrowed as many as he could, including *Robinson Crusoe*, *Pilgrim's Progress*, *Aesop's Fables*, and *The Arabian Nights*. The first book he owned and reread many times was *Life of Washington* by Parson Mason Weems.

In 1828, when Abraham was nineteen, his sister Sarah died while giving birth to her first child. In April of that same year, Lincoln left the family farm to help his friends Allen and James Gentry transport a flatbed of farm produce down the river to New Orleans. There Lincoln witnessed his first slave auctions, where black men and women were sold and their families broken up as they were auctioned off. This, plus his parent's anti–human bondage views, no doubt influenced Lincoln's later stand against slavery.

After Lincoln returned to Indiana, he moved with his family first to central Illinois, ten miles west of Decatur, and later to Goose Neck Prairie in Cole County, where he helped his father farm. Besides splitting fence rails and planting crops, Abraham made plans to take another boatload of cargo to New Orleans. In the spring of 1831, he and a friend, Denton Offutt, traveled by flatboat down the Sangamon River as far as New Salem, where they ran into difficulty getting their boat over a waterfall. Thinking that the town would attract more business as boat travel increased, Lincoln decided to stay in New Salem and accept a job as a clerk in the general store rented by Offutt.

# The Road to the Presidency

During his years in New Salem, Lincoln's interest in politics grew. The general store had a wood-burning stove, around which workers gathered to discuss both local and national politics. The leading national politicians at that time were President Andrew Jackson, John C. Calhoun of South Carolina, John Quincy Adams of Massachusetts, and Henry Clay of Kentucky. Lincoln found that his views were similar to those of Clay, who spoke out in favor of strengthening the federal government by supporting internal improvements (expansion of steamboat and train travel), a protective tariff, and a strong national bank. He also argued against slavery, thinking that slaves should be freed and returned to Africa.

Lincoln was interested in the ways in which boat travel could be expanded on the Sangamon River, and decided to run for the legislature in 1832. He lost, polling 227 out of 300 votes cast in the New Salem precinct. In 1833, he was appointed postmaster of New Salem and also deputy county surveyor. These two jobs came along at just the right time, as the general store in which he worked had gone out of business,

1842

Marries Mary Todd
on November 4.

1843

Robert Todd is born
on August 1.

1844

Accepts William Herndon
as his law partner.

as had a second store he had purchased with the help of
William F. Berry, a preacher's son.

During the time Lincoln worked as a store clerk, he
improved his education by studying mathematics, reading
the poetry of Robert Burns and Shakespeare, and polishing
his writing by poring over the *Kirkham's Grammar* book.

By 1834, Lincoln was eager to run for the legislature again
and, at age twenty-five, was elected to the Illinois House of
Representatives. Encouraged by this success, he decided to
take up the study of law and, after teaching himself from
borrowed law books, received his law license in 1836.
Described by friends as a serious bookworm with an inex-
haustible curiosity, Lincoln was also known for moodiness
and spells of depression. When his good friend Ann
Rutledge died in 1835, Lincoln was especially despondent—
leading some people to believe that Ann was more than
just a friend.

In 1836, 1838, and 1840, Lincoln was reelected to the
Illinois General Assembly and moved to Springfield, Illinois,
the new home of the capital. Besides becoming a partner in
the law firm of John T. Stuart, and later partnering with
Stephen T. Logan, he also started courting his future wife,
Mary Todd. At age twenty-one, Mary was lively and outgoing,
and particularly enjoyed discussing politics at the parties that
both she and Lincoln attended. Her family frowned upon
the courtship, since they looked down on Lincoln's humble
roots and frontier accent. After the couple became engaged,
Lincoln broke off the relationship because of intense pressure

1846

Edward Baker is born on March 10.
Lincoln gets elected to the United
States House of Representatives on
August 3.

1850

"Eddie" dies on February 1.
Lincoln's third son, William
Wallace ("Willie"), is born on
December 21.

1853

Thomas ("Tad") is
born on April 4.

from Mary's family. Remarking on the Todd family, Lincoln said that one *d* was enough to spell God. But it took two *d*'s to spell Todd.

Lincoln and Mary suffered from being apart. In 1842, however, over her family's objections, Mary Todd married Lincoln on November 4.

During the first eighteen years of their marriage, the Lincolns remained in Springfield and had four children. Lincoln established a new law practice and hired a junior partner named William H. Herndon. He traveled extensively in the Ninth Judicial Circuit, covering more than 400 miles throughout the state of Illinois and gaining a reputation as an outstanding lawyer.

In 1854 Lincoln decided to run for the U.S. Senate. His decision to reenter politics was determined partly by his opposition to the Kansas-Nebraska Act, supported by Stephen A. Douglas. Passed in 1854, the bill allowed the settlers in the new western territories, including Kansas and Nebraska, to decide for themselves whether or not they would embrace slavery. This was in direct violation of the line established in the Missouri Compromise passed thirty-four years earlier, in which only the new states south of the line could determine whether or not to be slave states.

Lincoln was outraged by the Kansas-Nebraska Act, referring to slavery as a "monstrous injustice" and a violation of the right of man to govern himself as set forth in the Declaration of Independence. Although he was defeated in the election by Lyman Trumbull, his views on slavery impressed the

| | | |
|---|---|---|
| Runs for the U.S. Senate. | Is defeated in his race for U.S. Senate. | Gives over 50 speeches in support of John C. Frémont, the Republican presidential candidate. |

new Republican Party in Illinois, and he campaigned heavily for the Republican presidential candidate, John C. Frémont. He also spoke against the Dred Scott decision, passed in March of 1857, which removed the right of Congress to exclude slavery from new western territories. Instead, the government's duty was to protect the rights of property owners, including the right to own slaves.

In 1858, Lincoln ran for the U.S. Senate for a second time, and engaged in a series of seven famous debates throughout Illinois with his opponent, Stephen A. Douglas. On the night of his nomination, Lincoln delivered his famous "House Divided" speech, in which he stated: "We are now far into the fifth year, since a policy was initiated, with the avowed object, and confident promise, of putting an end to slavery agitation. Under the operation of that policy, that agitation has not only, not ceased, but has constantly augmented. In my opinion, it will not cease, until a crisis shall have been reached, and passed. A house divided against itself cannot stand. I believe this government cannot endure, permanently half slave and half free." Again, Lincoln lost the election, but two years later he had another opportunity to challenge Douglas. In 1860, the Republican Party nominated Lincoln as their presidential candidate. His democratic opponent was Stephen A. Douglas.

Douglas stood for "popular sovereignty," the right of the western territories to decide for themselves whether or not to adopt slavery. Lincoln, as before, felt that slavery should be outlawed in the new territories. But he also did not see how

| 1857 | 1858 | 1860 |
|------|------|------|

Speaks out against the Dred Scott decision.

Runs for the U.S. Senate against Stephen Douglas. Gives his famous "House Divided" speech. Is defeated by Douglas on November 2.

Nominated for president at Republican Convention on May 18 and elected on November 6.

slavery could be abolished in the Southern states that already practiced slavery, without destroying the unity of the Union. His policy was that slavery should be contained in the states that already had it, and prevented in future states that might join the Union. He hoped that in time, the institution of slavery would weaken and eventually die out. Described in the South as a "lunatic," a "nigger lover," and a "baboon," Lincoln nevertheless received the majority of popular votes and was elected president of the United States on November 6. Six weeks later, South Carolina seceded from the Union, followed by Mississippi, Florida, Alabama, Georgia, Louisiana, and Texas. Deciding to form a nation of their own, this collection of states called itself the Confederacy and named Jefferson Davis as president.

On April 12, 1861, Confederate soldiers opened fire on Fort Sumter in Charleston, South Carolina. The Civil War had begun.

# The Presidential Years

At first, Lincoln's goal as president was to find a way to reunite the country. He did not think it wise to take a strong stand against slavery, as it would anger those Southerners who, he hoped, wanted to preserve the Union as much as he did. In addition, he thought that if the government were to take an active antislavery position, the neutral border states would fall to the South. As the war progressed, however, he realized

**1861**

Inaugurated as the 16th president of the United States on March 4. Fort Sumter attacked by Confederate soldiers on April 12. The Union troops lose the Battle of Bull Run on July 21.

**1862**

Willie Lincoln dies of typhoid fever on February 20. Confederate Army defeated in Battle of Antietam on September 17.

that the Southern states cared more about slavery and independence than they did about the Union. By firing on Fort Sumter, for example, Confederate rebels had shown that South Carolina wanted no part of the Union.

Hoping to swiftly defeat the rebels, Lincoln ordered 75,000 militia to get ready to defend the Union. Virginia, alarmed that federal troops would be advancing on Southern territory, quickly seceded on April 17, followed later by North Carolina, Tennessee, and Arkansas. There were now eleven Confederate states, and the border states of Maryland, Missouri, and Kentucky were threatening to secede as well.

Although the commander at Fort Sumter surrendered to the rebels before Lincoln could dispatch troops, Lincoln was convinced that the North must continue to make plans to defeat the Southern rebellion. The federal government, however, was plagued by a lack of capable generals to train its army. Winfield Scott, the general in chief of the Union Army, had not fought since the Mexican War of 1847 and was too elderly to fight in the field. He was also handicapped by inexperienced junior officers. Simon Cameron, the secretary of war, and his small staff had the difficult job of organizing the Northern regiments into a strong army. Cameron also had to address the issue of Northern black men who wanted to fight for their country. By federal law, blacks were not allowed to join state militias, even though they had served in the Revolutionary War and the War of 1812. The administration described the war as a white man's war, a war to save the Union, not to free the slaves. (After the Emancipation

**1863**

Issues the Emancipation Proclamation on January 1. Signs a bill creating a national banking system on February 25. Delivers the Gettysburg Address on November 19.

**1864**

Chooses Ulysses S. Grant as general in chief of Union Armies. Elected to a second term as president on November 8.

Proclamation, Congress finally authorized blacks to enlist in the Union Army. All in all, 200,000 enlisted and 38,000 were killed or wounded while distinguishing themselves on the battlefield.)

In the first eighteen months of the war, the Union troops suffered a number of humiliating defeats: the Battle of Bull Run on July 21, 1861; the Battle of Shiloh on April 6–7, 1862; the Seven Days Battles from June 25 through July 1, 1862, in which both sides suffered heavy casualties; and the Second Battle of Bull Run on August 29–30, 1862. Lincoln blamed these defeats partly on the inadequacy of his generals. George B. McClellan, for example, always seemed to come up with excuses not to fight—his men needed more time to train, he needed reinforcements, and so on. General George Gordon Meade was ordered by Lincoln to attack General Lee's troops in northern Virginia, but Meade procrastinated, protesting that he could not find Lee's exact position. About his reluctance, Lincoln remarked, "It is the same old story of this Army of the Potomac. . . . Imbecility, inefficiency—don't want to *do*. . . . It is terrible, terrible, this weakness, this indifference of our Potomac generals, with such armies of good and brave men. . . . What can I do with such generals as we have? Who among them is any better than Meade?" Not all of Lincoln's generals, however, disappointed him. General Ulysses S. Grant distinguished himself in Tennessee when he captured first Fort Henry and then Fort Donelson in February 1862, earning the nickname "Unconditional Surrender" Grant.

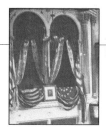

**1865**

Inaugurated as president on March 4. Confederate General Robert E. Lee surrenders to General Ulysses S. Grant at Appomattox Court House, Virginia. On April 14, assassinated by John Wilkes Booth while attending a play at Ford's Theatre and died the next morning. Buried at Oak Ridge Cemetery in Springfield on May 4.

As the war progressed, Lincoln was pressured by abolitionists and liberal Republicans alike to issue a decree to end slavery once and for all. Frederick Douglass, a black abolitionist in the North, argued forcibly that ending human bondage should be a war objective. Senator Charles Sumner argued that if Lincoln emancipated the slaves, the Confederacy would lose its labor force, forcing it to surrender. And General John C. Frémont, who was in charge of organizing an army to fight the Confederates in Memphis, Tennessee, went so far as to proclaim that all slaves in Missouri were henceforward free. Furious that Frémont had overstepped federal authority, Lincoln was forced to dismiss him. However, despite his public stance that the North was fighting to preserve the Union, Lincoln was privately against slavery. As the war ground on and it became clear that the Confederate states wanted to hold onto slavery at all costs, his views changed. On July 21, 1862, Lincoln told his cabinet that he wished "to take some definitive steps in respect to military action and slavery." The next day, he shared an early draft of the Emancipation Proclamation, in which he stated that by January 1, 1863, as commander in chief of the army and navy, he would liberate all slaves in the rebel states. But first, he hoped for a major Union victory to bolster the government's strength.

It came with the Battle of Antietam on September 17, 1862, when General George McClellan finally took action and stopped General Robert E. Lee's armies from moving further north through Maryland toward Washington. It was the bloodiest battle of the war, with 26,000 men wounded, dead, or missing. Even though another Union loss followed— in the Battle of Fredericksburg on December 13—Lincoln issued the final draft of the Emancipation Proclamation on January 1, freeing all slaves held by the Confederates and allowing black soldiers to enlist in the Union Army.

Despite more defeats, the Union Army triumphed in the Battle of Gettysburg, July 1–3, 1863, and in the Battle of Vicksburg, July 4, 1863. On November 23–25, 1863, General Ulysses S. Grant achieved a Union victory at the Battle of Chattanooga and became the general in chief of the Union Army. But it took two more grueling years of fighting for the Union to win the war. Finally, on April 9, 1865, General Robert E. Lee surrendered to General Ulysses S. Grant at Appomattox Court House in Virginia.

Meanwhile, Lincoln was reelected president after running against former General George B. McClellan, and made a famous inauguration speech: "With malice toward none; with charity for all . . . let us strive on to finish the work we are in . . . to do all which may achieve and cherish a just, and a lasting peace, among ourselves, and with all nations."

On April 14, 1865, four years after the beginning of the war and only a little more than a month after his reelection, President Abraham Lincoln was shot in the head while attending the play *Our American Cousin* with his wife Mary at Ford's Theater in Washington. Assassinated by John Wilkes Booth, an actor loyal to the South, he died at 7:22 A.M. the following day in a house across the street.

On December 6, 1865, the Thirteenth Amendment was passed by Congress, abolishing slavery.

# Home and Family

Lincoln was admired by many for his honesty, courage, and intelligence. His wife, Mary Todd Lincoln, on the other hand, was unpopular. She was considered to be spoiled, immature, insecure, and extravagant. People laughed at her behind her back. Still, when she and her future husband were courting, Lincoln found her a lively conversationalist. She could talk on many subjects, from poetry to the theater to politics. At five feet two inches, Mary was more than a foot shorter than her husband, and a good deal plumper. She found Lincoln refreshingly different from the other men in Springfield, and was attracted to his looks.

Lincoln described himself as "in height, six feet, four inches, nearly; lean in flesh, weighing, on an average, one hundred and eighty pounds; dark complexion, with coarse black hair, and grey eyes." Although the Civil War was a strain on their marriage, they were holding hands moments before Lincoln was killed.

The Lincolns had four children: Robert Todd Lincoln, born August 1, 1843; Edward "Eddie" Lincoln, born March 10, 1846; William "Willie" Wallace Lincoln, born December 21, 1850; and Thomas "Tad" Lincoln, born April 4, 1853. One of the great tragedies of the Lincoln's marriage was that their three youngest boys all died before reaching adulthood. Eddie died at age three from what was described as diphtheria. Willie died at age eleven, apparently from typhoid fever. A lover of books like his father, Willie's loss was felt keenly by both parents. Tad Lincoln was perhaps the most mischievous of the boys. While living at the White House, he was known to break mirrors, interrupt cabinet meetings, and perform pranks of all kinds. After his father's death, Tad moved with his mother to Chicago and attended the Brown School, where he became editor of the newspaper. In 1869, he and his mother went to live first in Germany and then in France. On the ocean voyage home, Tad caught a cold which worsened into tuberculosis. He died at age eighteen on July 15, 1871.

Mary and the president adored their boys and enjoyed their jokes. They did not discipline them very much, preferring instead to spoil their children. Mary Lincoln suffered terribly at the deaths of her three youngest sons, and after Lincoln's assassination, she was tormented by grief on and off for the rest of her life. Terrified of being alone and of becoming poor, she spent lavishly on clothes and furniture. As a widow, her circumstances were vastly reduced, leading to further misery. People made fun of her for hearing voices and attending séances. Finally, concerned for her health, her oldest son, Robert, ordered an insanity hearing, in which he testified against her. After ten minutes of deliberation, the jury committed her to a sanitarium, where she stayed for four months. When she was released, she lived with her sister for almost a year before a second jury concluded she was "restored to reason and capable to manage and control her estate." Mary never forgave Robert for testifying against her. She died from what was probably a stroke on July 15, 1882.

Robert grew up to be a successful lawyer. He was appointed secretary of war under President James Garfield and served as minister to England under President Benjamin Harrison in 1889. Later in life, he became the acting president and chairman of the board of the Pullman Company before retiring with his wife and three children to his estate, Hildene, in Manchester, Vermont. He died on July 15, 1926.

If you are interested in learning more about Lincoln, the

Civil War, or the subject of slavery, please visit our interactive Web site at winslowpress.com, where you will find a separate Web site for the *Dear Mr. President* series as well as a separate home page for each of its books.

Here also is a list of books for further reading:

# Books written for kids

Freedman, Russell. *Lincoln: A Photobiography.* Boston: Houghton Mifflin, 1987.

Marrin, Albert. *Commander in Chief: Abraham Lincoln and the Civil War.* New York: Dutton Books, 1997.

Cox, Clinton. *Forgotten Heroes: The Story of the Buffalo Soldiers.* Demco, 1993.

Meltzer, Milton, ed. *Lincoln: in His Own Words.* Florida: Harcourt Brace, 1993.

Murphy, Jim. *The Long Road to Gettysburg.* New York: Clarion Books, 1992.

Rappaport, Doreen. *Escape from Slavery.* New York: Harper Trophy, 1991.

Rutberg, Becky. *Mary Lincoln's Dressmaker Elizabeth Keckley's Remarkable Rise from Slave to White House Confidante.* New York: Walker and Co., 1995.

# Books written for adults

Carpenter, Francis B. *The Inner Life of Abraham Lincoln*.
Boston: Houghton Mifflin, 1983.

Donald, David Herbert. *Lincoln*. New York: Touchstone
Books, 1996.

McPherson, James. *Battle Cry of Freedom: The Civil War Era*.
Oxford: Oxford University Press, 1988.

Nicolay, John G. and Burlingame, Michael. *An Oral History of
Abraham Lincoln: John G. Nicolay's Essays and Interviews*.
Southern University Press, 1994.

Oates, Stephen B. *With Malice Toward None: A Life of Abraham
Lincoln*. New York: Harperperennial Library, 1994.

Sandburg, Carl. *Abraham Lincoln: The Prairie Years and The
War Years*. Florida: Harcourt Brace, 1989.

Stern, Phillip Van Doren, ed. *The Life and Writings of Abraham
Lincoln*. New York: Modern Library, 1999.

# Books that kids and adults can enjoy

Fehrenbacker, Don E., ed. *Abraham Lincoln: Speeches and Writings 1932–1958 (vol. 1) and 1859–1865 (vol. 2)*. New York: Library of America, 1989.

Haskins, Jim. *Black, Blue and Gray: African Americans in the Civil War.* New York: Simon and Schuster, 1998.

Hurmence, Belinda. *Slavery Time When I Was Chillun.* New York: G.P. Putnam's Sons, 1997.

Jacobs, Harriet, writing as Linda Brent. *Incidents in the Life of a Slave Girl.* New York: New American Library, 2000.

Kunhardt, Peter W., Philip B. Jr., and Philip B. III. *Lincoln: An Illustrated Biography.* New York: Gramercy, 1999.

Meltzer, Milton, ed. *Frederick Douglass: In His Own Words.* San Diego: Harcourt Brace and Company, 1995.

Meltzer, Milton, ed. *Lincoln: In His Own Words.* San Diego: Harcourt Brace and Company, 1995.

Here is a reproduction of an actual letter from Abraham Lincoln to Charles Sumner, written on May 19, 1864.

Executive Mansion,

Washington, May 19., 1864.

Hon. Charles Sumner.
        My dear Sir:
                The bearer of this
is the widow of Major Booth,
who fell at Fort-Pillow—
She makes a point, which I
think very worthy of considera-
tion which is, widows and children in fact, of colored soldiers who fall in our service,
be placed in law, the same
as if their marriages were legal,
so that they can have the bene-
fit of the provisions made the
widows & orphans of white soldiers.— Please & hear Mrs.
        Booth.
                                Yours truly
                                A. Lincoln

Lettie Tucker's letters might have looked something like this:

Dear H.;                    March 10, 1862

Near a month has passed,
and I have not heard from
you. I know you are a busy
man being the president, so
I will not pester you. Has
thinking on your high-hattin'
life affected you so badly?
Yours for true,

Lettie

Tucker Plantation
Charleston, South Carolina

# The U.S. Postal Service, 1861–1863

Lettie Tucker sent her letters to President Lincoln through the U.S. postal service. Around the time of their correspondence, lots of changes were going on in the way mail was delivered, since many different techniques were being put into practice.

Postage stamps were introduced in 1847. The image of Benjamin Franklin was on the five-cent stamp, and George Washington was on the ten-cent stamp. In 1863, a single rate system was set up so that no matter how far your mail was going, it cost the same amount. Also in 1863, a free delivery service was established to forty-nine cities across the country, and the mail began to be sorted into three different classes: first class for letters, second class for magazines and newspapers, and third class for all other mail.

The delivery technique itself went through some big changes in the 1860s. The famous Pony Express was established in the early part of the decade as a fast way to move mail. Young men rode cross-country on horseback delivering the mail by relay in just ten days. Prior to this, the same trip could take as long as three weeks by stagecoach. The Pony Express continued until the first telegraph line was completed in 1861. The traveling post office, another experimental program, was introduced in 1862. Mail was sorted in special train cars while in transit in order to save time. This proved to be quite successful and, although people eventually stopped working on the trains, rails remained the most popular way for mail to move cross-country until the number of passenger trains was reduced and the highway post office service overtook it in 1941.

# Interactive Web Footnotes

Here is an alphabetical list of the interactive footnotes found at the bottom of the pages in this book. We hope that this list will prove to be an easy reference for locating the subjects you are interested in at this book's own Web site at **winslowpress.com.**

Abolitionist movement
African Americans in Philadelphia in the 1800s
Attack on Fort Sumter
Causes of the Civil War
Children in the White House
Christmas during the Civil War
Daily life on a plantation
Edwin M. Stanton
Election of 1862
Emancipation Proclamation
Frederick Douglass
Generals of the Civil War
How slave families were split apart
Laws preventing slaves from reading and writing
Life in the South after the Emancipation Proclamation
Lincoln's children
The Lincolns' pets
Lincoln's religious beliefs
Lincoln's speech at the 1858 Republican Convention
Major battles of the Civil War
Mary Todd Lincoln
Northern, border and rebel states

# Index

*(Colored numbers represent photographs or illustrated material)*

## A

## B

# E

# F

# G

# H

# I

# J

# K

# L

# M

# N

# T